This Christmas story
is dedicated to my family
My wife Ali , Harry & Laura;
Love you always D.
and to all families
who believe in Father Christmas.

Christmas time is a
time for being together and sharing;
and if you know anyone
who is spending Christmas alone
give them a call,
send them a card and let
them know that you are
thinking of them at this special time.

It was a cold winters night, the wind was blowing hard, the sleet was stinging Abigale's face as she tried to shield herself and hold the hand of her little boy James; as they walked along the dark paths towards their broken little cottage that was just inside the woods,

Abigale knew when they got home it would be cold and dark as there was no one else to light the wood fire for her, on the way they saw a poor old lady struggling to cross the road in the dark, she had only managed to get a quarter of the way across the road before she was struck and knocked down by a big black coach with six black horses pulling like a train,

Abigale screamed as the old lady was sent spinning across the wet dirty road, her little wicker basket spilling its contents in to the puddles, Abigale told her son to hang on to the nearby gas lamp and stay put.

The coach and horses had stopped and a footman jumped down from the Coach and looked briefly and shouted "don't worry, it's just an old peasant woman" Abigale ran towards the old lady and knelt down to hold her head, she tried to give her comfort, the old lady looked up at Abigale's face and looked deep into her watery eyes, she held Abigale's hand tightly and began to whisper,

Abigale could hardly hear her, "come closer child" she said, the old woman pushed her purple velvet scarf into Abigale's hand and began to chant some words that Abigale was unfamiliar

with, just then James cried out "mummy help me", Abigale saw a cloaked figure with a top hat trying to take James away.

The old woman shouted "go to him now,"

Abigale ran across the road nearly being hit by another team of horses going the other way, when she got there the gentleman was well to do, he had a kind but familiar face, he said "I was concerned the boy was lost young lady" Abigale said "no I was trying to help the old lady over there in the road" he said "did she give you a scarf by any chance, a purple scarf?"

Abigale said "why yes she did." Abigale turned to look at the old lady but she was no longer there, she had completely disappeared. The gentle man in the top hat said "this happens every third night before Christmas eve, it happens every ten years, only those who are kind of heart can see her, she has bestowed a lifelong gift to you for trying to help her, the gift can come at any time in your life but you will know when it does, good night my dear oh I forgot to tell you, the purple scarf, you must wear it now."

Abigale put the scarf on and by the time she had wrapped it around her neck the man in the top hat a disappeared too. Abigale was very confused, as they got to the edge of the woods they could see the outline of their broken little cottage by the moonlight, but as they got closer they could see smoke coming out of the chimney, and lights at the windows and a big Christmas tree with decorations all around, their broken cottage was not broken anymore, in fact it looked brand new.

Abigale threw the front door open and saw the old lady's basket on the kitchen table and it was full of gold coins and a note saying "you and your son will never be cold, hungry or poor ever again." It was the gift, the gift from the old lady and Christmas Past.

Abigale had just put James to bed on Christmas eve, she had just finished reading him his favourite Christmas bedtime story, she sat on the edge of James's bed looking at his happy little face and thinking how lucky they both had been a couple of nights ago.

The fire had burnt down in the hearth to red glowing embers and the warmth radiated across the room, James was so excited because it was Christmas day tomorrow, Abigale kissed him gently on his forehead and a piece of James blonde curly hair stuck to her lip and they both giggled, Abigale then said goodnight sleep well James, then as she walked across the room to blow out the candle ; James watched her shadow on the bedroom wall get bigger as she reached the candle, one puff and it was nearly completely dark except for the red embers of the fire.

James shut his eyes tightly as Abigale turned to check on him just once more. Abigale then went to get ready for bed herself. She put her clothes on the chair at the end of her bed and hung her purple velvet scarf on the back of the bedroom door; she jumped into her bed and could just about see James's little face poking out of his covers. Not but an hour had passed when all of a sudden there was a loud windy, blowy whistling noise, it was so loud it woke them both up, the curtains were flapping about like the wings of a big dragon.

Abigale had to shout quite loudly "Are you OK James? " James was loving the experience, he was laughing his head off, he wasn't scared at all, suddenly the purple velvet scarf blew off from the hook from the back of the door and landed on the end of James's bed; it seemed to be moving like a snake, it wriggled from one side of his bed and then back again it then seemed to wiggle its tail at James as if to say "follow me"

James shouted across the room at his mum," "your scarf is alive" it then wiggled on to the floorboards and then very unexpectedly began to slide between a gap in the floor, Abigail leapt out of bed like a jack in the box and just managed to get hold of the last corner of the scarf as it was disappearing.

It was so strong Abigale lost her grip and the scarf had gone "OH NO, NO, NO, NO." Shouted Abigale," "now what am I going to do?" " James sat up in bed and simply said "We must go after it mummy, it was your Christmas gift" and with that being said Abigale pulled back the floor rug to reveal a rather large trap door that was never there before, it had a big round brass ring handle and embossed on the handle were the words pull me.

They both tugged at the big brass handle and slowly but surely the big trap door made a huge creaking noise and began to slide open. "THERE IT IS" shouted James, "your scarf mummy your scarf it's on the top step"

Abigail grabbed an oil lantern and lit it, when she held the lantern over the trap door opening, they both gasped in amazement, the hole was huge the staircase was made of thick oak and lead down to the beginning of a slide also made of polished oak, suddenly another gust of wind blew the scarf down the steps and on to the slide and it was gone with a whoosh.

"Come on Mummy let's go" shouted James, and wearing only their pyjamas they climbed down the staircase until they got to the top of the slide, "STOP" Abigail shouted, "there's a sign" "what does it say?" said James, " it says, when using the slide it will make you smile but look out for the flying crocodile!"

"That sounds very dangerous, they have sharp teeth". Said James, Abigail said "right I'll get on and you sit on my lap and you hold the oil lamp. One, two, three and we're off," "Weeeeeeeeeeeeeeeeeeeeee" they both shouted with joy as the wind rushed through their hair.

The slide went up and down and round and round and they were going faster and faster, "Crackety Crack, Snappity Snap," "what's that noise mummy?" James asked, "don't look behind us but it's a flying crocodile, and he's chasing us down the slide," "Snappity Snap, Crackety Crack" went the crocodiles teeth, the crocodile swooped down onto the side but his sticky feet made such a screeching noise he scared himself and flew off the other way.

"Phew that was close" said Abigail, eventually the slide began to level out and in front of them was a small hole in the wall and they both shot through it with almighty "POP".

They eventually stopped sliding, and saw a sparkly door with a sign saying "This Way".

They held the oil lamp high up as they pushed the door open with lots of effort, inside the room it was dark and they could see what looked like a big sleigh, it was very old and very dusty, "MUMMY LOOK" shouted an excited James "there's your scarf and it's polishing the dust off".

Suddenly the walls were sparkling with diamonds and the room got brighter and brighter in fact it got so bright they had to shield their eyes, once their eyes had got used to the light they could see the sleigh in all its glory, it had silver runners and a red outer body, plush green leather seats and silver bells all around it, but sitting on the seat was a dark black cloak and a top hat. James stared at it and said "who do they belong to Mummy?

Before Abigail could speak, there was a booming "HO, HO, HO welcome to my home," the face, it was the familiar face Abigail remembered seeing one Christmas eve as a child, it was Father Christmas himself, he said "tonight I needed some help to get this sleigh flying and you two were my only hope because you believe in me, you can help deliver the presents to all the families with me tonight", just then the big sack of present appeared out of thin air and the reindeer walked into the sparkling room.

Clippety cloppety clippety clop, all the reindeer looked very smart, they were each wearing their harnesses that were a beautiful red colour, and there were tiny little bells sewn all along them, their eyes were as bright as a soldiers buttons and their fur was groomed perfectly; all eight reindeer lined up side by side and then walked gently backwards until Father Christmas could attach the reins to them all.

James could not stop smiling; he was sniffing the gorgeous smell of the freshly polished leather and was so excited to see real live reindeer and of course Father Christmas. As soon as they were hitched up Father Christmas checked the big red bag of presents was tied on to the sleigh properly with the golden threaded rope. Father Christmas said "Well I think we are ready now, climb aboard." Abigale and James stepped forward holding hands, Abigale helped James climb into the Sleigh, "That's right James you sit next to me" said Father Christmas.

Abigale climbed in to the sleigh and sat next to James so he was safe in between them. Once they were comfortable, Father Christmas pulled a big brown furry blanket over their knees, it was nice and soft and very warm; James was wriggling with excitement. Father Christmas said "you are the first young man to have a ride in this sleigh since I was five years old the same as you are now when I had ride with my grandfather" James was smiling and Father Christmas ruffled James's hair with his big red mittens.

"Walk on" boomed Father Christmas, the reindeer took the strain of the weight of the sleigh their harnesses creaked and the sleigh began to move slowly towards the wall in front of them, James said "How are we going to get out of this room?"

Father Christmas lifted his right arm up in the air and slowly made the shape of a rainbow, and as he did that; the same shape appeared in the wall and Abigale and James sat there with their mouths wide open as they looked ahead and saw what looked like a tunnel, there was deep snow on the ground and tall trees lined the way, the trees tops had curved over towards each other almost touching at the top. The reindeer started picking up speed and some snow was being kicked up in the air as they started to go faster and faster. Abigale put her arm round James and held him tightly, the moon was shining bright tonight and it was flickering through the tree tops as they dashed along; the sound of the sleigh in the snow made a swishing noise as they went sliding through the snow.

Suddenly the noise stopped, it went very quiet as the sleigh gradually left the ground, they got to the end of the tunnel and the reindeers legs were going really fast, "UP WE GO" shouted Father Christmas and the reindeer pulled them high into the moon lit sky with the sound of jingle bells ringing as they went.

The wind was blowing everyone's hair about, at one point James grabbed hold of Father Christmas's beard because it flapped up over his nose. As they travelled along Abigale and James looked down and could see the town below, the river sparkled as the moonlight danced on the water and made it shimmer in the light.

Father Christmas said "We must look out for the factory chimney pots they seem to be getting taller each year, as they got nearer the town James could smell a smoky smell, they must be getting close to the chimney stacks of the factories; the smoke was getting stronger, and then it was getting thicker, it got so thick it was very difficult to see, then all of a sudden there was a mighty chimney pot stack in front of them, "GO LEFT. GO LEFT" shouted Father Christmas and the reindeer all leaned over to the left just in time as they flew past it at high speed, "OH NO GO RIGHT GO RIGHT" Shouted Abigale as they whizzed past another tall chimney stack just missing it by the whisker of a field mouse, James shouted "YOU HAVE GOT SOOT IN YOUR BEARD" and he laughed and that made Father Christmas laugh too, Father Christmas said, "don't worry about that James, you should see me at the end of the night HO, HO, HO".

The smoke had been that thick, no one had noticed that they had lost height and were flying lower than they thought they were, all of a sudden the lead reindeer on the left clipped his front hoof on the top of the factory building, the sleigh started to slow down and loose more height, luckily they had just came out of the thick smoke and Father Christmas could see one of his reindeer had hurt his ankle. "Oh no we are going to have to stop and to see if he is alright" Said Father Christmas, the moon was shining brightly and Father Christmas could see a farm in the distance, it was on the other side of the river and behind a tall hedge, gradually they got lower and lower and were getting close to the river, the sleigh dipped down suddenly as the lead reindeer couldn't pull any more, they were losing power, skimming the river; the runners of the sleigh sprayed water thirty feet up in to the night sky.

"We're not going to make it over the hedge" Shouted Abigale, "FLY REINDEER FLY, PLEASE FLY" shouted James who was feeling a little bit scared, the lead reindeer tried his best to start running again but he really was in a lot of pain, the sleigh climbed higher and they just made it over the top of the tall hedge, they could hear the blackbirds chirping angrily as they were woken up by the sleigh rustling through the top of the hedge, soon Father Christmas managed to land in a field behind the farmhouse.

They all got out of the sleigh and went to see the poor reindeer that had hurt his ankle, it didn't look good, and his poor ankle was swollen. In the corner of the field they could see an old stable the door was hanging off and the windows were broken, but Father Christmas said to the poor reindeer, "we will leave you hear in that stable and collect you when we have delivered all the presents, so James, Abigale and Father Christmas helped the poorly reindeer to the old stable, they just got inside when they heard some movement in the straw,

"Who's there?" said Father Christmas, and from out of the dark corner in the stable slowly walked a very old grey donkey, his eyes looked sad, he looked very lonely, but when the donkey saw the poorly reindeer he walked forward and rubbed his big old nose on the reindeers neck, he knew he wasn't well, the donkey pointed with his nose towards to corner from where he came and there was his old straw bed, the donkey took the reindeer to his bed as if he was trying to tell him to rest for a while.

Suddenly Father Christmas had an idea and said to Abigale "do you have your purple velvet scarf with you?" Abigale said "yes it's in my pocket of my pyjamas, do you need it?" Father Christmas nodded slowly and took the purple velvet scarf and tied it around the old donkeys neck, he then rubbed his neck and whispered something in his big floppy ear.

The donkeys eyes lit up and he nodded his head up and down as if he had understood every word. Father Christmas said to the donkey "What is your name?" and "how old are you?" James giggled and said "Donkeys can't talk" "ahem" the donkey cleared his throat and said,

"My name is Danial, I am nearly 50 years old, I have been working on the farm for all of those years and now I am too old to work and my owners are going to sell me." James and Abigale once again had their mouths wide open in disbelief. Father Christmas said "well we need your help tonight Danial, will you help us?"

Danial said" I would love to help you but I am just too old." Father Christmas said "well you were too old; but since you have been wearing the magic purple velvet scarf I have given you back 30 years of your life."

Danial the Donkey walked out of the stable and in to the moon light and sure enough his eyes were bright, his fur was not grey anymore but a rich chestnut brown and his hooves were strong as ever.

They took Danial the Donkey to the sleigh and attached the harness to him. Danial said "wait a minute, I can't fly," Father Christmas said "as long as you keep that purple velvet scarf on you can do anything." All of a sudden Danial the donkey let out the biggest, longest and loudest EEEAW anyone had ever heard before, "Shush" Said Father Christmas, "you will wake everybody up," they looked back at the farm house and could see the curtains moving and small children looking out of the bedroom window.

Father Christmas waved his arm in the air again and as if by magic delivered the presents to the farmhouse in a flash. Danial started running with the other reindeer and they took off again with all the bells ringing, it was an eventful night delivering all those presents around the world from England to America, to Australia and India, they visited every home on the planet, on the way back they stopped off at the farm and said goodbye to Danial the Donkey but that was not all.

Father Christmas waved his arm in the air and pointed at the Stable and before their eyes the stable gradually began to look new again Just like Abigale's cottage had, and who should come walking out of the stable but the poorly reindeer.

Father Christmas took the purple velvet scarf off of Danial's neck and wrapped it around the reindeers hurt ankle. Suddenly there was a little eeeaw sound coming from the stable.

Danial said "Who's there?" and a girl Donkey came walking out and said "I am your new best friend and you will never be lonely ever again, the two donkeys and the reindeer rubbed noses to say goodbye to each other, all the presents had been delivered on time; they made it back to Abigale's cottage just before sunrise.

Father Christmas gave them both a big hug and said you better both get to bed now as there are some presents I have to deliver on my own, and of course he meant presents for Abigail and James.

Christmas morning had arrived; Abigail awoke to see her purple velvet scarf hanging on the bedroom door and James still asleep in his bed, had it all been a dream? Had Abigail imagined it all? She got out of bed and saw the biggest heap of presents in her life, she lifted the floor rug to look for the trap door and fell backwards with surprise and fell on her bottom with a thud, the trap door was still there with a note on it saying "until next Christmas eve" James jumped out of bed and gave Abigail her purple velvet scarf back and said "I think you may need to wash this mummy, and Merry Christmas," they both hugged each other and from that day; every Christmas eve they helped Father Christmas deliver the presents although neither of them were very keen on the flying crocodile,

"Snappity Snap, Crackety Crack"

"Snappity Snap, Crackety Crack"

"Snappity Snap, Crackety Crack"

Merry Christmas

The end

Author Derek Crysell

Printed in Great Britain
by Amazon